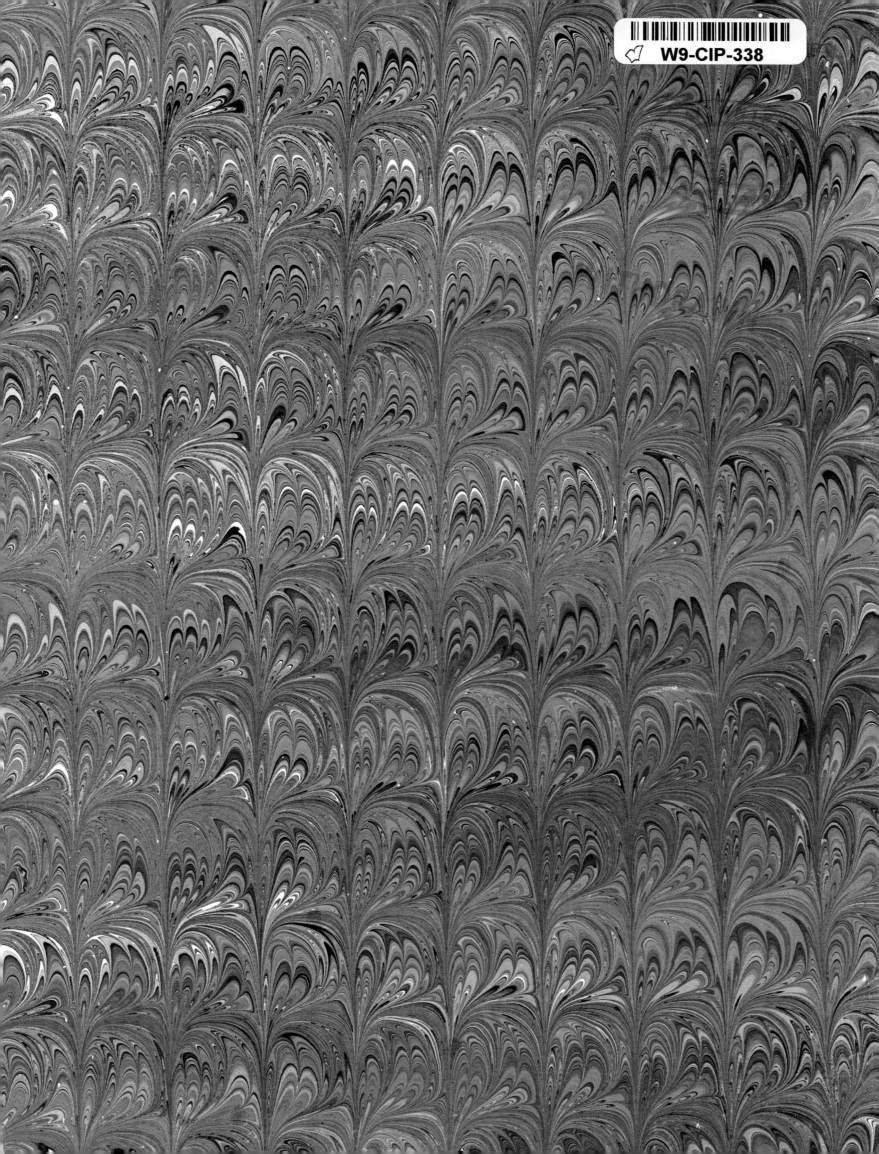

BELIEVE ME, LORDS AND LADIES, IT'S A RULE

THAT BRAINY PEOPLE LOVE TO PLAY THE FOOL.

HIERONYMUS KARL FRIEDRICH, BARON MÜNCHHAUSEN
1720-1797

THE WONDERFUL TRAVELS
AND ADVENTURES

OF

Baron Münchhausen

AS TOLD BY HIMSELF IN THE COMPANY
OF HIS FRIENDS, AND WASHED DOWN
BY MANY A GOOD BOTTLE
OF WINE

THE ADVENTURES ON LAND

ILLUSTRATED BY BINETTE SCHROEDER
TEXT BY PETER NICKL
TRANSLATED INTO ENGLISH BY
ELIZABETH BUCHANAN TAYLOR

NORTH-SOUTH BOOKS
NEW YORK

First published in the United States
and Canada in 1992 by North-South Books, an imprint of
Nord-Süd Verlag AG, Gossau Zürich, Switzerland.

Copyright © 1977 by Nord-Süd Verlag AG, Gossau Zürich, Switzerland
English text copyright © 1979 by Chatto & Windus Ltd.

First published in Great Britain,
Australia and New Zealand in 1979 by Chatto & Windus Ltd.
Reissued in 1992 by North-South Books, an imprint of
Nord-Süd Verlag AG, Gossau Zürich, Switzerland.

Library of Congress Cataloging-in-Publication Data is available

British Library Cataloguing in Publication Data
Schroeder, Binette
The wonderful travels and adventures
of Baron Münchhausen.
1. Nickl, Peter 2. Taylor, Elizabeth Buchanan I. Title
833'.9'1J PZ7.S3797

ISBN 1-55858-134-0

1 3 5 7 9 10 8 6 4 2
Printed in Belgium

I SET OFF ON MY JOURNEY TO RUSSIA IN THE
MIDDLE OF WINTER, KNOWING FULL WELL THAT
the roads leading through the northern part of Germany,
through Poland, Kurland and Lithuania, must all be covered
with snow and ice. Indeed, according to the reports of travellers
who had gone before me, the roads were quite exceptionally bad
that winter, even more difficult than the road to the gate of
heaven.

I was journeying on horseback, which is always the most
convenient method of travelling provided that both horse and
rider are in good temper. At least one doesn't risk an *affaire
d'honneur* with one of our genteel German postmasters, nor is
one obliged to stop at every tavern for one's continually thirsty
postillion.

Unfortunately I was but lightly clad, which I found the more
uncomfortable the further north-east I rode. Imagine, then,
how a poor old man must have suffered, whom I came across on
a bleak wasteland in the most desolate countryside of Poland.
He lay helplessly shivering, with practically no means of cover-
ing his nakedness. I pitied the poor soul from the bottom of my
heart, and although my own body was almost numb with cold, I

5

threw my winter coat over him. At that same moment a voice rang out from heaven, praising this heroic deed and saying, 'My son, may the Devil take me if I do not reward you for this!'

I RODE ON UNTIL NIGHT and darkness overtook me. Nowhere was a village to be seen, nor any sound to be heard. The whole countryside lay covered with snow, and I could not tell which way to go. Tired of riding, I descended from my horse and tied him to a sort of pointed tree-stump that was protruding above the snow. For safety's sake I tucked both pistols under my arm, then lay down not far from my horse and slept so soundly that my eyes did not open until another bright, light day had dawned. But imagine my astonishment when I saw that I was lying in a graveyard in the middle of a village. My horse was at first nowhere to be seen, but then I heard him neighing somewhere up above me. Looking in that direction I saw that he was tied fast to the weather-cock of a church steeple and was dangling precariously from it. I knew in an instant what had happened. The village had been covered in snow during the night but the weather had suddenly turned, and I myself had sunk gently down during my sleep with the melting snow into the graveyard, and what I had in the dark taken for the stump of a young tree, to which I had tied my horse, was in fact the cross or weather-vane of the church steeple.

Without further ado I took one of my pistols, shot at the halter, and so brought my horse back down to the ground, and thence proceeded on my journey.

I TRAVELLED EASILY AND COMFORTABLY astride my horse until I reached Russia. However, since it is not the fashion there to travel on horseback I submitted, as I always do, to the custom of the country and took a small horse-sleigh, with which I drove briskly on to St. Petersburg.

I do not remember now whether it was in Estland or Ingermanland, but it was in the middle of a dark forest somewhere that I suddenly caught sight of a fearsome wolf who was pursuing me with all the fury of his raging winter hunger. He was about to overtake me, and there was no possibility of escape. Instinctively I lay down flat on the floor of the sledge and let my horse work for us both, and to our mutual advantage.

What I had been counting on, and yet had hardly dared hope or expect, happened. The wolf was not in the least interested in my own paltry figure, but jumped straight over me, fell savagely upon my horse and instantly tore into the hind-quarters of the poor animal, who ran all the faster for pain and terror.

Perceiving that I was still alive, I lifted my head cautiously and saw with horror that the wolf had fairly eaten the hind legs off the horse and was already almost inside him. I seized my opportunity and beat the wolf furiously with the whip. Such an unexpected attack in the rear frightened him so much that he charged forward with all his might, the horse's carcass fell to the ground, and the wolf now found himself in the harness where the horse had been. For my part I did not cease to flog him, and so we arrived in St. Petersburg at full gallop, much against our mutual expectations and to the not inconsiderable astonishment of the onlookers.

8

GENTLEMEN, I DO NOT want to bore you with the politics, art, science, or even the history of this magnificent city, but I would think it a great pity if my readers were kept in ignorance of the story of the great songstress Gabrielle. I heard her once in St. Petersburg and was enchanted. I hurried over to her, threw myself at her feet and begged her to give me one of her high 'C's! After all, I did offer her 100 Louis-dors for it! She consented at last and presented me with one of her highest and most beautiful trills. It was so divine that I straightaway preserved it in spirit, and believe me, it continues to delight me to this day. By Jove, what a trill it is!

Nor do I want to tire you with the intrigues and escapades of those belonging to the politer circles of that country, where the lady of the house always receives visitors with a dram and a hearty kiss. And so I shall confine my narrative to things of a great and noble sort, such as horses and dogs — I have always been a great friend of both — and also foxes, wolves and bears, with which Russia is more bountifully endowed than any other country on earth. It is in gallant adventures that a gentleman's true worth is proven and this has always been more to my fancy than all that musty Greek and Latin, or even all the sweet perfumeries and fineries of our French fops and hairdressers.

It was some time before I could take up my commission in the army. For a couple of months I was my own master, and in a position to squander both my money and my time in the most honourable fashion. This I did freely, as you can imagine, but always well away from the city, and in the company of bold fellows who knew how best to enjoy such a wild, undeveloped hunting territory. Even now I look back fondly to this time, to its diversity of amusements and to the extraordinary good luck I had in bringing off some of my bolder endeavours.

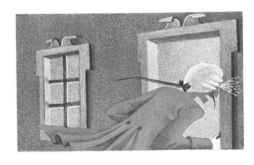

LOOKING OUT ONE morning through my bedroom window I saw a large pond which lay not far off. It was strewn with wild ducks. Instantly I took up my rifle and leapt down the stairs so precipitately that I ran headlong into the door-post. Fire, sparks and stars flashed before my eyes, but didn't in the least distract me from my purpose. I was soon ready to shoot; however, as I lined myself up for the kill I discovered that the violence of the blow had forced the flint out of my gun. There was no time to lose. Remembering the effect of the shock on my eyes, I tore the pan out and took aim at the wild ducks, my fist clenched before one of my eyes. The hefty blow that followed scattered sparks into the powder; the shot went off, and amazingly I gunned down a dozen ducks, four widgeons and a couple of small teals.

ON ANOTHER OCCASION, WHILE ON A HUNTING expedition, I spied a dozen wild ducks swimming across an inland lake. Unluckily I had only one shot left in my gun and so could not hope to slay more than a single bird. I would fain have had them all, for I could have entertained a good few friends with these, and with great festivity.

Then I recollected that I had a small piece of bacon in my game-bag, a remnant from my own supplies. I attached this to a

11

long dog-lead which I had by me, which I unravelled and thus lengthened by at least four times. Thereupon I hid myself in the bulrushes on the shore, flung the morsel of meat towards the pond and watched with great pleasure as the nearest duck raced over and devoured it. The others followed on the first one's heels, and since the greasy scrap on the end of the string emerged almost unchewed from the first duck, it was gobbled up by the next one, and so on by each duck in turn. In short, the morsel travelled whole through each and every one of the ducks, without becoming detached from its thread. Soon they were all strung together like pearls on a necklace. With great satisfaction I drew them into the shore, slung the necklace over my shoulder and set off for home.

SINCE MY HOUSE WAS STILL A GOOD WAY OFF, and the burden of such a bevy of ducks became increasingly wearisome, I nearly came to regret having caught so many. But then such an extraordinary thing happened that I was thrown into a great quandary. The ducks, being indeed still very much alive, began, as soon as they had recovered from their initial shock, to beat furiously with their wings and took off into the air with myself dangling below. Now some would have found this an exceedingly tricky situation. But I turned the circumstance

as best I could to my advantage, by using my coat-tails to steer myself through the air in the direction of my house. When I arrived above it I was able to let myself down without injury. By manoeuvring the head of first one duck and then another I descended slowly and gently, and to the great astonishment of my cook, through the chimney of my house and on to the hearth where, fortunately, there was no fire burning.

A SIMILAR EXPERIENCE befell me once with a flock of hens. I had gone out in order to test a new gun, and had spent all my supply of grape-shot, when to my surprise a flight of hens soared up from under my feet. The desire to see some of these on my table that very same evening kindled in me such inspiration as you, gentlemen, could turn to good account in times of similar fortune. As soon as I had determined where the hens had come to rest I swiftly loaded my gun — not, however, with ordinary ammunition but with the ramrod, the far end of which I sharpened to a point, as best I could being in such a hurry. Thereupon I advanced towards the hens, pulled the trigger — whereat they flew up in terror — and had the great pleasure of seeing my ramrod slowly sink down in the distance strung with seven hens, who might well wonder at finding themselves harpooned together so.

SUCH A MASTER-STROKE DOES NOT ALWAYS succeed, and on occasion even the best-aimed shot fails to reach its target, but very often chance and good luck can make up for such mishaps. I can tell of one such incident which is quite

unique of its kind. Finding myself one day in the very wildest of hunting territory, I caught sight of a young boar, and a sow running close on its heels. My shot missed them both. The young boar ran on; the sow, however, stood motionless, as though rooted to the ground. On investigating further I found that the sow was blind with age, and was clenching the boar's tail in her teeth, ready to be led forward like a docile child. But my bullet had struck between the two animals and had torn through this leading-rein, one end of which the sow was still guarding preciously. Since her guide was now no longer pulling her forward, she had come to a standstill. I took hold of what remained of the young boar's tail and led the helpless old animal homewards, without further difficulty on my part, the sow having not the slightest suspicion of anything untoward or offering the least resistance.

TERRIBLE THOUGH THESE SOWS ARE, FAR MORE fierce and dangerous are the older boars. On one occasion when, unhappily, I was prepared neither for attack nor defence, I came across one of them in the middle of a wood. I sprang instinctively behind the nearest tree, as the furious beast pounded towards me and with the weight of his whole body levelled a side-thrust at me. This would certainly have done me no good at all, for it was delivered with such force that the beast's tusks pierced right through the tree-trunk; the boar, for his part, was not in a position to retract his tusks, let alone repeat the attack. Ho ho! I thought, I'll get you now! and I took up a stone and hammered and beat at his tusks in such a manner that there was no possibility of his escape. And so he had to wait patiently while I went to the nearest village and fetched a cart and a rope with which to tie him up securely and convey him alive and in good condition back home.

16

Presence of mind is often the father of heroic enterprises. Soldiers and sailors not infrequently owe a timely escape to quick wits, and the huntsman some rich spoils. Let me tell you of one such adventure.

ON A WELL-TENDED preserve in Russia I chanced upon a most magnificent black fox. To have shot through his valuable hide would have been a great shame. It so happened, however, that Reynard was standing right before a tree, and so I removed the bullet from the barrel of my gun and replaced it with a strong hammering nail. Then I fired, and my aim was so spot-on that I pinned his brush firmly to the tree. I ran over to him and with my hunting-knife slit straight across his face, then taking hold of my whip I flogged him carefully right out of his skin, which amused me greatly and was indeed a wonder to behold.

GENTLEMEN, YOU HAVE DOUBTLESS HEARD THE story of Saint Hubert, holy saint and protector of sportsmen and hunters, and of the splendid stag he once encountered in a wood, who bore the holy cross between his antlers. I have every year offered up my sacrifice to this Saint Hubert, and in good company, and have seen that very same stag painted on the walls of a thousand churches, so that on my honour as a huntsman I cannot say whether such stags have always existed or, indeed, whether they still exist to this day.

But let me tell you of something that I saw with my very own eyes. Having spent all my shot, I came quite by chance across

18

the most magnificent stag in all the world. He looked me straight in the eye as though he knew that I had no ammunition. Hastily I loaded my barrel with gunpowder and strewed over it a good handful of cherry stones which, as quickly as was possible in the circumstances, I had stripped of their flesh. And so he received the full force of this load right between his eyes. The shot stunned him somewhat, he staggered, but finally took to his heels.

A couple of years later I was hunting with a party of fellows in that very same wood, when behold! a stately stag appeared, with a most beautiful, fully-grown cherry tree between his antlers. The tree stood over ten feet high and was richly laden with cherries.

Recollecting immediately my earlier adventure, I looked upon the stag as my own well-deserved property, and with one shot brought him down. I can say therefore, on my honour, that with a single shot I acquired both some fine venison and a good helping of cherry sauce, each more delicious of its kind than any other that I have tasted before or since.

Who knows but that some pious huntsman, or a sporting abbot or bishop, may not have shot and planted the cross on Saint Hubert's stag in just the same way? Were not these gentlemen famed for their planting of crosses and antlers and, indeed, are they not so to this day?

BUT WHAT DO YOU THINK OF THE FOLLOWING case? I was in a Polish wood one day when both daylight and

powder ran out on me. As I groped my way home a terrible bear came hurtling towards me, his jaws open and ready to devour me on the spot. In great haste I ransacked my pockets for powder and lead — but to no avail. I found nothing but two remaining flintstones. I hurled one of these with all my might into the beast's open mouth and down his throat. This caused the monster such pain that he turned about, and I was able to fling the other stone between his hind legs. It was a master-stroke. Not only did this second stone penetrate right into his body, but it met up in his stomach with the first one, and kindled a great fire, so that with an almighty roar the bear exploded into two pieces.

Although I escaped unscathed that time, I would not like to repeat the experience, and even today would not wish to encounter a bear similarly unarmed.

IT SEEMS THAT I AM FATED TO MEET WITH THE wildest and most dangerous beasts when I am the least prepared for them, as though some instinct had told them of my defencelessness. On one such occasion I had just unscrewed the flint from my gun in order to sharpen it, when suddenly I heard the fierce growl of a bear next to me. I could only shin with all speed up a tree in order to prepare myself there for battle. Unluckily, during this operation my knife had fallen to the ground and now I had nothing with which I could fasten the screw, which was hard to turn. Beneath the tree stood the bear, and with every moment that passed I feared he would come after me. What should I do? I looked longingly after my knife, which stood upright in the snow. But the most anguished of gazes did

nothing to help the situation. Eventually an inspiration struck me, which was as extraordinary as it was opportune. I discharged a great stream of water, of which one always has an abundant supply in times of terror, and in such a direction that it hit exactly upon the hilt of my knife. The abominable cold of Russia froze the water immediately and very soon a beam of ice had formed above my knife which, to my great good luck, reached as far as the lower branches of the tree. With great haste I grasped the end of the pole and so was able, without much difficulty, but exercising infinite care, to draw my knife up towards me. Hardly had I screwed the flint fast when Bruin began to mount the tree. Truly, I thought, one would have to be no wiser than a bear to let slip such an opportunity, and I delivered my ursine friend such a heartily-felt salute that he forgot about tree-climbing forever.

BUT WHAT ABOUT THE FOLLOWING STORY? I came upon a wolf at such proximity, and so unexpectedly, that I had no alternative but to follow a mechanical instinct and ram my fist down his throat. For my own safety I reached further and further in until my arm disappeared almost up to the shoulder inside his gullet. How could I get out of this one? I cannot say that I particularly enjoyed being in this predicament. What can one do, when face to face with a wolf, but tremble? We eyed each other none too lovingly. Had I withdrawn my arm the beast would only have sprung at me with all the more vigour — that much was plain from his raving eyes. Without further ado I seized hold of his intestines, pulled, and turned him inside out like a glove, whereupon I flung him to the ground and left him.

THIS SAME EXPEDIENT would not have succeeded, however, against a mad dog which came tearing towards me soon after in a narrow alley in St. Petersburg. Run while you can! I thought, and threw off my coat to facilitate my flight. I reached home in one piece. Shortly afterwards I sent my servant out to fetch the coat and bade him hang it in the wardrobe beside my other clothes. The next day I was startled, and at the same time amused, when Johann uttered a piercing shriek. "For God's sake, Baron," he cried, "your coat's gone mad!" I hastened to the spot. The boy was right. I found all my clothes strewn about the place and torn to shreds, and with my own eyes I saw how the mad overcoat fell upon my best dress-suit and mercilessly shook it to pieces.

FROM ALL THESE DILEMMAS, GENTLEMEN, I escaped only by the skin of my teeth, and with not a little luck — but remember, it was only because of my quick wits and, indeed, courage that I was able to turn the situation to my advantage. These two qualities together are, as everyone knows, the stuff of which soldiers, sailors and huntsmen are made. But it would be a poor fellow indeed who always depended on good fortune and his stars, without having practised the finer skills of his profession, and without equipping himself with the best implements possible with which to achieve success. Such a reproach could never, however, be levelled against me — to this day I am renowned for the excellence of my horses, dogs, swords and other weapons, as well as for the masterly way in

which I apply them, so that I may justly hope that my name will be remembered in the forest, on the turf and in the field.

I do not want to embarrass you with details of my stables or kennels, or even of my array of armaments, as so many fashionable huntsmen are wont to do. But I must draw your attention to two of my dogs whom I loved particularly. One was a whippet, the other a pointer of such ceaseless energy that everyone who saw him envied me. He served me both day and night; when darkness fell I hung a small lantern from his tail and could hunt as well if not better than in full daylight.

IT WAS WITH THE HELP OF THIS SAME POINTER that I was able to solve a mystery which might otherwise have perplexed me to the end of my days. I had been after a hare for two days. My dog had chased him tirelessly but I could never get close enough to shoot. I have never believed in magic, having myself experienced such extraordinary fortunes, but I didn't know what to make of this matter. Eventually, however, I pulled off a shot. He fell to the ground, and I was amazed at what I saw. My hare had four legs underneath his body and four more on top. When the lower pair was tired he flipped himself over like one of those clever swimmers who can swim as well on their backs as on their fronts, and charged on at still greater speed on the new pair.

28

I HAVE NEVER AGAIN ENCOUNTERED SUCH A hare, and would certainly not have caught this one were it not for the uncommon zeal of my dog. He would to this day be the most notable representative of his species were it not for that whippet of whom I spoke earlier, who was also well deserving of this honour. The whippet, a bitch, grew up in my household, and was remarkable not so much for her form as for her quite astounding swiftness. If you had seen this animal, my friends, you would have been amazed, and would not have wondered that I set such store by her when hunting. She ran so fast and so long in my service that her legs wore down to mere stumps under her body, so that towards the end of her life she was of use only as a terrier. But even in this capacity she served me well for many a year.

WHILE STILL A WHIPPET, HOWEVER, SHE ONCE set after a hare which seemed to me uncommonly large. I was sorely afraid for my poor bitch. She was heavily pregnant and yet hunted as keenly as ever. I could only follow at some distance on my horse. Suddenly I heard a yelping as though from a pack of hounds, but such light and high-pitched barks that I did not know what to make of them. On reaching the spot I almost fell off my horse in wonder. The hare had given birth while running, and my bitch had produced also, and there were

as many small leverets as pups. By instinct the former ran, and the latter chased after, and finally were able to hunt them down. And so I found myself at the end of the course in possession of six hares and as many dogs, although I had begun the day with only one of each.

I REMEMBER THIS BITCH WITH AS MUCH pleasure and affection as that marvellous Lithuanian horse, whose value far exceeded my own pocket. Nevertheless he came into my possession, and under the most fortunate of circumstances, which at the same time gave me the opportunity to demonstrate my exceptional skill in riding.

It happened one day in Lithuania on the magnificent estate of Count Przobfsky. I was taking tea with some ladies in the salon. The gentlemen had gone out into the courtyard to inspect a young thoroughbred horse which had just arrived. Suddenly we heard a cry for help. I raced down the stairs and found the horse behaving so wildly that nobody dared to approach him, let alone attempt to mount him. Even the most fearless of riders stood aghast and terrified, and dismay was evident on every face. I leapt with one jump into the saddle, and by this surprise attack was able to tame the horse. Using all the skill I could muster I coaxed the animal into obedience and good temper. Wanting to impress this upon the ladies, and above all, of course, to protect them from further shock, I dug my heels in and we leapt through the open window of the salon. There we continued the course, and rode up and down many times, walking, trotting and even galloping. Finally I brought my horse to rest on the tea-table, where I made him repeat his lessons *en miniature*, to

the great delight of the ladies. He went through his paces without faltering and broke not a single cup or pot.

And so I gained the favour not only of the ladies but also of the noble count, who with his customary courtesy made me a present of this young horse and begged that I would accompany him to victory in the field. The campaign against the Turks was soon to be opened under the command of the Count of Münnich.

I COULD NOT HAVE RECEIVED A MORE agreeable present nor, indeed, a more auspicious one at the beginning of that campaign, in which I served my apprenticeship as a soldier. A horse as gentle as he was strong — at once a lamb and a Bucephalus — he not only awakened in me the virtues of the gallant soldier but also reminded me of the duties of the gentleman on the field, and even inspired visions of the young Alexander and the astonishing feats he accomplished in battle.

Among other reasons, it seemed, we took to the field in order to redeem the reputation of the Russian army, which had suffered somewhat during Tsar Peter's last Prussian campaign. This goal we achieved several times over, for we fought many strenuous battles under the command of the aforesaid general, and with glorious results.

Modesty forbids the ordinary soldier to attribute to himself particular successes or victories. The honour is usually reserved for the generals or, what is worse, for the kings and

queens, who have never caught a whiff of gunpowder, except at field days and reviews of their troops, and who have never even seen a battlefield, much less a hostile army.

For my own part I would not make any particular claims to the glory we achieved in military confrontations. We all did our duty. Every patriot, soldier and nobleman knows the import of this simple idiom, and what measure of honour, glory and achievement it implies. The crew of idle intellectuals and coffee-house politicians know nothing of duty, or have only the meanest conception of it.

Be that as it may — I had meanwhile taken command of a regiment of hussars and had led several attacks of some importance, and modesty cannot, in all conscience, prevent me from crediting the success we achieved in these expeditions to my own account and to that of the dauntless company of soldiers whom I led to conquest and victory.

IN OCZAKOW WE HAD A very hard time of it, being in the front line against the Turks. My fiery Lithuanian horse had led me into the devil of a stew. I was positioned well in advance and saw the enemy charge towards me in such a cloud of dust that I could assess neither their actual strength nor their true intentions. To conceal myself in a similar cloud of dust was an easy trick, but would not have helped me much, nor advanced the cause for which I had been sent out. Therefore I let my horses out on both the right and the left flank to stir up all the dust they could. I myself rode straight on towards the enemy, not least in order to get a better view of them, which I was indeed able to do. But not for long, however, for the Turks, who had at first boldly stood their ground, now began to scatter in sheer panic at the sight of my horses. This was the moment to launch the attack. We broke them entirely and dealt them such a crushing defeat that they were not only forced back to their stronghold but out through the other side, against even our most hopeful expectations.

OWING TO THE EXTRAORDINARY SWIFTNESS OF my horse I had been foremost in pursuit, and now I watched with great pleasure as the enemy fairly flew through the opposite gate. I thought it advisable then to pull up in the market place and for trumpeters to call for a rendezvous. Imagine, then, my astonishment when I saw neither trumpeters nor any one of my hussars around me. Were they scouring the other streets? Had some misfortune befallen them? They could not be far away and must soon catch up with me. And so I waited, and meanwhile guided my panting horse to the spring in the market-place so that he might refresh himself. He drank greedily and with a thirst that was not to be quenched. But this was natural enough, gentlemen, for what did I see when I looked behind me? The entire hind-quarters of the poor creature were missing, croup and legs included, as though they had been chopped off. And so the water ran out as fast as he drank it, without refreshing him in the least.

How this had come about remained a mystery to me, until my groom came hurrying over and informed me amidst peals of laughter and violent curses of what had happened. As I charged headlong with the routed enemy into the fortress they had suddenly dropped the portcullis on me, thereby cutting the poor animal in half. The hind part had been pounced upon by the enemy and had suffered the most terrible ravages, but then had gallantly picked itself up and fled to a nearby wood, where with luck it was still to be found.

I TURNED ABOUT immediately and, galloping peculiarly fast on the remaining half of the animal, I rode over to the meadow. To my great joy I found the other half waiting here, and to my even greater astonishment saw that it was amusing itself with the sport of a true *maître de plaisir,* with all the keenness possible in a headless creature. In short, the rear half had wasted no time in making the acquaintance of the mares of the chase, and the pleasures of his harem seemed to have put all thoughts of discomfort out of his mind.

HAVING SUCH INDISPUTABLE PROOF THAT there was still life in both halves of my horse, I immediately summoned the farrier. Without much hesitation he stitched the two parts together with some young laurel shoots which were near at hand. Fortunately the wound healed, and caused the most amazing thing to occur, which could only have happened to such a horse. The shoots sprouted roots in his body, which grew upwards and formed an arbour around me, so that I was able thereafter to ride gloriously out in the shade of my own laurels — and those of my horse, of course.

I WOULD MENTION IN passing yet another adversity arising out of this incident. I had cut at the enemy with such prolonged vigour that I found my right arm rising and falling in a perpetual cutting motion. I could not check this tendency even now that the enemy was well and truly despatched. So as not to strike myself or indeed my men inadvertently, I was obliged to wear my arm in a sling for a full eight days, as though it had been half lopped off.

YOU CAN DOUBTLESS IMAGINE, MY FRIENDS, how a gentleman such as myself, in possession of a horse such as my fiery Lithuanian, could indulge in yet more equestrian acrobatics. On one occasion, when we were laying siege to a town in the north-west, I was able to demonstrate a masterly command of horsemanship. It appeared exceedingly difficult, even impossible, to penetrate through all the outposts, bastions

and sentry guards of the fortress to see how matters stood there. Spurred on by an almost immoderate devotion to duty I had positioned myself next to a large cannon which was then fired directly into the fortress, and in a trice I sprang on to the cannonball, hoping thereby to gain an entrance into the stronghold. But half-way through the air all sorts of doubts occurred to me. Hm, I thought, you may get in, but how will you get out again? And what might befall you once inside? You'll be taken for a spy and hung from the nearest gallows. It was not a comfortable thought. Thinking quickly, as only a few yards away from me a cannonball flew out from the fortress towards our own camp, I leapt from my missile on to this other one, and though without achieving my purpose, I returned safe and sound to my own dear people.

IN THOSE DAYS, GENTLEMEN, I WAS SO LIGHT OF heel, as was my horse, that neither ditches nor fences ever prevented us from taking the shortest route possible. I was once coursing a hare. A coach containing two ladies drove by, and passed directly between me and the hare. Without deviating from our course or scraping even a corner of the carriage, we leapt straight through it. What luck that both windows were open! It happened so quickly that I hardly had time to raise my hat to the ladies and humbly to beg their pardon for the liberty I had taken.

ON ANOTHER OCCASION I WANTED TO CROSS A quagmire which, when already in full flight, I discovered to be much wider than I had at first thought. Still hovering in mid-air, I turned and retreated to where I had come from, in order to take a bigger leap. But again I fell short of the opposite bank, and plunged up to my neck in the swamp. Here I would undoubtedly have perished were it not for the force of my arm pulling on my hair-plait which pulled me out again, together with my horse whom I was holding tightly in the grip of my heels.

DESPITE MY VIGOUR AND COURAGE, AND THE speed of my horse, my efforts in the Turkish campaign were not always successful. I even had the misfortune to be overpowered by numbers, to be taken a prisoner of war, and what was worse, to be sold as a slave, a practice still common among the Turks. I lived in a state of extreme humiliation. My daily tasks were not really hard or strenuous, but rather strange and irksome. I had to drive the Sultan's bees out to the meadow each morning, keep watch over them all day long, and in the evening bring them back to their hives. One evening I was missing a bee, and very soon I discovered that two bears had fallen upon her, ready to tear her to pieces for the small drop of honey she carried. I had no weapons to hand save for my silver axe, the tool of the

44

Sultan's guards and farmers. I hurled this after the robbers in order to frighten them and set the bee at liberty, but by an unfortunate turn of my arm the axe flew upwards, and flew, and flew until it reached the moon and came to rest there. How could I now recover it? What ladder on earth would stretch that far?

I remembered then that Turkish beans grow very quickly and rise to amazing heights. I planted one immediately. It grew upwards and soon curled itself round one of the moon's horns. Now I was sure of my plan — all I had to do was to climb up towards the moon, which I reached safe and sound. Since everything glistens like silver there it was a hard task to discover where my axe had fallen. Eventually, however, I found it amongst a pile of chaff and straw.

Now I had to climb down again, but alas! The heat of the sun had completely dried up my bean. A thin thread remained which was hardly strong enough to take my weight. I was at a loss for what to do. I did not hesitate for long, however, but straightaway set about plaiting a rope out of straw, as long and as strong as I could make it. I fastened it round the moon's horn and proceeded to let myself down by it. With my left hand I held tightly on to the rope and in the right I clutched the axe. When I had slid a fair way down I cut the now useless upper part of the rope with my axe and tied it to the lower end, and thus continued my journey down. But this repeated splicing and tying did not make the rope any stronger, nor did it quite bring me down to the Sultan's farms.

I WAS STILL SUSPENDED in the clouds and a good few miles from *terra firma* when all at once the rope snapped and I fell with such violence to the ground that I found myself stunned, and buried in a hole nine fathoms below the surface. When I re-emerged I could see no-one, far or near, who might help me. There was nothing for it but to go home myself and fetch a spade, and then carefully dig myself out layer by layer. I managed to do this even before the Sultan's watchmen had discovered my long absence.

WITH THIS EXPERIENCE BEHIND ME I WAS NOW better able to deal with the bears, who were still ravaging my bee for her drop of honey. I spread some honey on the narrow shaft of a haycart and lay down not far from it. My expectations were fulfilled. An enormous bear approached, enticed by the smell of honey, and began to lick so greedily from the head of the pole down that it rammed straight through his throat, stomach and abdomen and out the other end. Now that he had so conveniently licked his way on to the pole and thus impaled himself, I ran up and stuck a peg through the hole in the end of the shaft,

48

thus blocking the bear's retreat, and left him standing there till the next morning. The Sultan, who chanced to be passing on his morning walk, laughed till he cried at this affair.

SOON AFTERWARDS PEACE WAS CONCLUDED with the Turks, which despite the efforts of French politicians was very favourable to Russia. I regained my freedom and was sent back to Russia, but soon thereafter departed from St. Petersburg. It was at the time of that momentous revolution — some forty years ago now — when the Tsar, who was still in his cradle, his mother, and her father the Duke of Brunswick, along with Field-Marshal Münnich and many others, were sent to Siberia. The winter was exceptionally severe that year in Europe, and it seems to me that ever since that time the sun has suffered from a slight frostbite.

ONE CONSEQUENCE OF the frost sticks in my memory particularly, and could indeed be a case for philosophical speculation, gentlemen. I had had to leave my horse in Turkey and was travelling day and night by stage-coach. Suddenly we found ourselves driving down a narrow bridle-path which was hemmed in on all sides by a high thorn-hedge. I begged the postillion to sound a signal with his horn so that we would not collide with vehicles coming the other way. He immediately blew with all his might into the horn, but his efforts were in vain. Not a single note issued forth.

50

He did not know what to make of this, since he claimed to be an excellent performer, and it perplexed me too. Shortly afterwards we met with a coach coming in the opposite direction. This was tiresome for both parties, especially in view of the weather, and it was impossible for either coach to proceed. I had no alternative but to jump out of the cab, unyoke the horses and, taking the whole coach — wheels, baggage and all — upon my shoulder, to carry it over hedge and ditch. As you will understand, this was no mean feat, considering the weight of the carriage. Then I returned to the horses, tucked one under each arm and ferried them over in the same manner. When the other coach had driven by I transported horses and carriage back to the road and harnessed the yoke again, whereupon we proceeded swiftly and comfortably until we reached the next inn, where we settled down in good spirits to a round of ale. The postillion hung up his overcoat and horn, sat down by the hearth and forgot his cares. I sat on the other side of the fire and did the same.

Now listen, gentlemen, to what happened next! Suddenly we heard a Tereng, Tereng, Tereng teng teng! We looked round in surprise and now saw clearly the reason why the postillion had not been able to sound his horn. The notes had frozen inside the horn and now, as they thawed out, rang loud and clear across the room, and to the credit of the blower. And so it came about that the merry fellow entertained us that evening with a great many melodies and cadences, without once putting the horn to his lips. We heard the 'Prussian March', 'Over Hill and Over Dale', and many other favourite songs, and even the lullaby, 'Now the Woods have Come to Rest'. With this last the thaw-concert ended, and here too, my friends, I shall end this account of my travels in Russia.

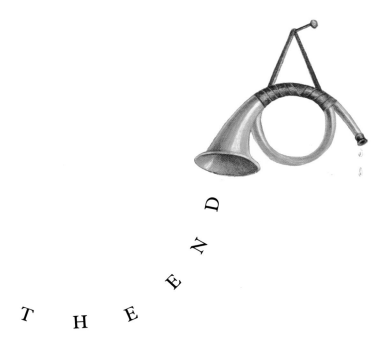

THE END

EPILOGUE

THE TALES OF MÜNCHHAUSEN

When the first account of Baron Münchhausen's adventures appeared in London in 1784 one English critic hoped that it would finally "lead to the taking of certain steps in Parliament". He thought the stories offered a good lesson to liars, and even recommended that the practice of "tall story-telling" be encouraged. Another critic went so far as to speak of the moral purpose of the tales.

Their theories were not altogether far-fetched. Münchhausen's tales were never concerned with personal glory, nor did he wish to boast, and certainly not to tell lies. If some braggart tried to get the better of him he would show him up by over-credulous remarks and even more exaggerated stories. The charm of his tales lies in the manner of recounting outlandish feats and incidents in a tone which implies that perhaps, after all, they are just possible.

Münchhausen gives us an insight into the high culture of story-telling of the rococo age. He invented and improvised in the manner of a true *raconteur* for the benefit of his friends. He did not achieve literary recognition in his lifetime and in his later years felt this to be sore insult to his honour. He was particularly bitter about the fact that tall stories were often published under his name regardless of their origin.

TABLE OF DATES

1720
Hieronymus Karl Friedrich, Baron Münchhausen, is born in Bodenwerder.

1736
Having for several years been a page in the service of Prince Anton Ulrich von Braunschweig-Wolffenbüttel, Münchhausen now enters the Russo-Turkish war as a member of the prince's dragoon regiment. It is the reign of Tsarina Anna (1730-1740), when Russian policy is almost exclusively determined by the country's German advisers. Anton Ulrich himself is married to the Tsarina's niece and, as father of the future Tsar Ivan VI, hopes to obtain a leading position in the Russian government. Count Münnich, later to become Prime Minister, is at this time a field-marshal.

1737
Münnich takes Oczakow by storm. This town, situated at the mouth of a river on the Black Sea, was one of the most important Turkish strongholds.
After the defeat of Oczakow Münchhausen is made an officer, and a year later becomes a lieutenant in the dragoon regiment.
1737 is the year of the birth of Rudolf Erich Raspe, who first recorded the Münchhausen stories in the English language.

1739
The Russo-Turkish war comes to an end with the Peace of Belgrade.

1740
Ivan VI, son of Anton Ulrich, is crowned Tsar while still a child. His mother acts as regent for him.

1741
A military revolt brings to power Tsarina Elizabeth (1741-1762), youngest daughter of Peter the Great. The "Tsar in the cradle" and his parents are sent into exile, and because of strong nationalist movements in Russia are followed by a host of German minions, among them Count Münnich.

1744
Peter III marries Sophia Augusta von Anhalt-Zerbst, later Catherine the Great. On the journey to St. Petersburg the bride and her mother stop a few days in Riga, where Münchhausen's regiment is stationed. During their stay it is Münchhausen's duty to command the guard of honour. On their departure he accompanies the two noble ladies to the town gate.
On 2 February Münchhausen marries Jacobine von Dunten, daughter of a judge. They live happily together for 46 years. There are no children.

1748

Birth of Gottfried August Bürger, who is later to translate the Münchhausen stories into English, adding some new ones of his own.

1750

In Riga Münchhausen is named Captain of the Russian cavalry. After this appointment he takes a long holiday from the army, goes to Germany and soon thereafter severs all his ties with the Russian administration. He devotes himself from now on to running his hereditary estate in Bodenwerder, the so-called 'castle', and to hunting and the breeding of dogs and horses, as well as entertaining friends and guests in his house with great conviviality. Frequently, too, he makes small journeys in the surrounding country. He is always a welcome guest at the Rühland tavern in Göttingen, where his personality and his skill at story-telling are famous.

1755

Raspe steals 600 valuable gold coins from the cabinet of the Count of Kassel, of which he was keeper, and flees to England.

1781

The 8th part of "Vademecum for Revellers" is published by August Mylius in Berlin. This collection of frivolous and entertaining tales includes 16 tall stories which are ascribed to a certain very clever fellow, one Mr M-h-s-n. The 9th part of the Vademecum follows in 1783 and contains two more such stories. Their authorship is unknown. There is some evidence that they were written by Raspe, but this is not certain.

1785

Raspe brings together 17 of the 18 Vademecum stories in a collection of travel tales, translates them into English and publishes them under the title of "Baron Münchhausen's narrative of his marvellous travels and campaigns in Russia". The place of publication is Oxford; the author remains anonymous.

The Münchhausen stories are arranged into the adventures on land and the adventures at sea. The land adventures include only those to do with the "Russian journey" and have now been considerably elaborated by Bürger. Unlike the sea adventures, these adventures on land are said for the most part to be authentic tales as told by Baron Münchhausen. The first sea adventures are not published until the 3rd edition of Raspe's work appears.

1786

An English student, the young Lord Lisburne, introduces this 3rd edition to Bürger, who translates the book into German, adding some further stories, and publishes it under the title of "Wunderbare Reisen zu Wasser und zu Lande, Feldzüge und lustige Abentheuer des Freyherrn von Münchhausen, wie er dieselben bey einer Flasche im Circel seiner Freunde selbst zu erzählen pflegt". The place of publication is apparently London. For reasons of his position Bürger's authorship remains anonymous. In 1788 a second, extended edition appears, coinciding with the fifth English edition. This volume contains many additional sea adventures which are no longer based on Münchhausen's own stories.

1794

Death of both Raspe and Bürger.
Münchhausen, whose wife had died in 1790, now marries the young Bernhadine von Brunn — according to his contemporaries "a very proper person". Very soon after the wedding he opens divorce proceedings against her since he fears not only that she will put a stop to his pursuit of pleasure but also that she might bear him a false heir.

1797

Death of Baron Münchhausen. He dies with a reputation as a suspicious and mistrustful old man. His lasting resting place is the village church of Kemnade, near Braunschweig.

GOTTFRIED AUGUST BÜRGER

It is almost certain that Bürger met Baron Münchhausen at some point while he was studying in Göttingen, a town with only 800 inhabitants. Münchhausen often visited the town from his estate in Bodenwerder, which was less than two days' journey away, and often stopped at the Rühland tavern where he would sometimes entertain the other guests with his stories. Bürger must have been fascinated and inspired by the story-telling, for the cavalry captain's tales exactly fitted his own romantic inclination to a national heroic literature. So it was natural that, having come across the English version of the Münchhausen stories, Bürger should have translated these in just one and a half months, at the same time adding further stories of his own, and then submit his work to the publisher Dieterich in Göttingen. Since it was not proper for a university professor of his time to publish tall stories Bürger was not named as the author. He must have been glad of this anonymity for the contemporary critics spoke of a 'miserable style' and hammered the book utterly. Today Bürger's translation and interpretation of the stories is considered 'congenial'.

Despite the critics the book was an enormous success with the public. The financial gain, however, went solely to the publisher. On delivery of his manuscript Bürger had unfortunately relinquished all his claims to a royalty as he already owed Dietrich some money.

RUDOLF ERICH RASPE

Raspe was gifted not only as a writer but also as a scientist. He fell from his station because of, as it was later delicately described, "fatal transgressions against the seventh commandment". As keeper of the coins and treasures belonging to the Count of Hessen-Kassel he had appropriated a collection of valuable gold coins in order to pay off his enormous debts. To avoid imprisonment he fled to England, which in those days had no treaty of extradition with Germany, and continued to live there for several years though in very restricted circumstances. At first he tried to find work writing for both English and German publishing houses, but was never satisfied with his working conditions. He therefore supported himself for some time by doing translations and giving language lessons, and finally by working as a geologist in a mining establishment. It was during this time that he wrote the story of Baron Münchhausen's travels in Russia, the so-called land adventures, without ever thinking that this small volume would become part of the heritage of world literature.

ABOUT THIS BOOK

This book contains the adventures of Münchhausen on land. The third edition of Raspe's work and the second edition of Bürger's have served as the basis for the present text. The stories of the "Schnaps General" and of the "Pointer Piel", both invented by Bürger, have had to be omitted for editorial reasons. Instead, the episode concerning the singer Gabrielle has been introduced, the only story from the Vademecum which Raspe did not incorporate into his narrative. This tale seemed to him not to fit with the hunting and war adventures because of its overtones of gallantry, and hence has, quite unjustifiably, only rarely been published and indeed almost forgotten.

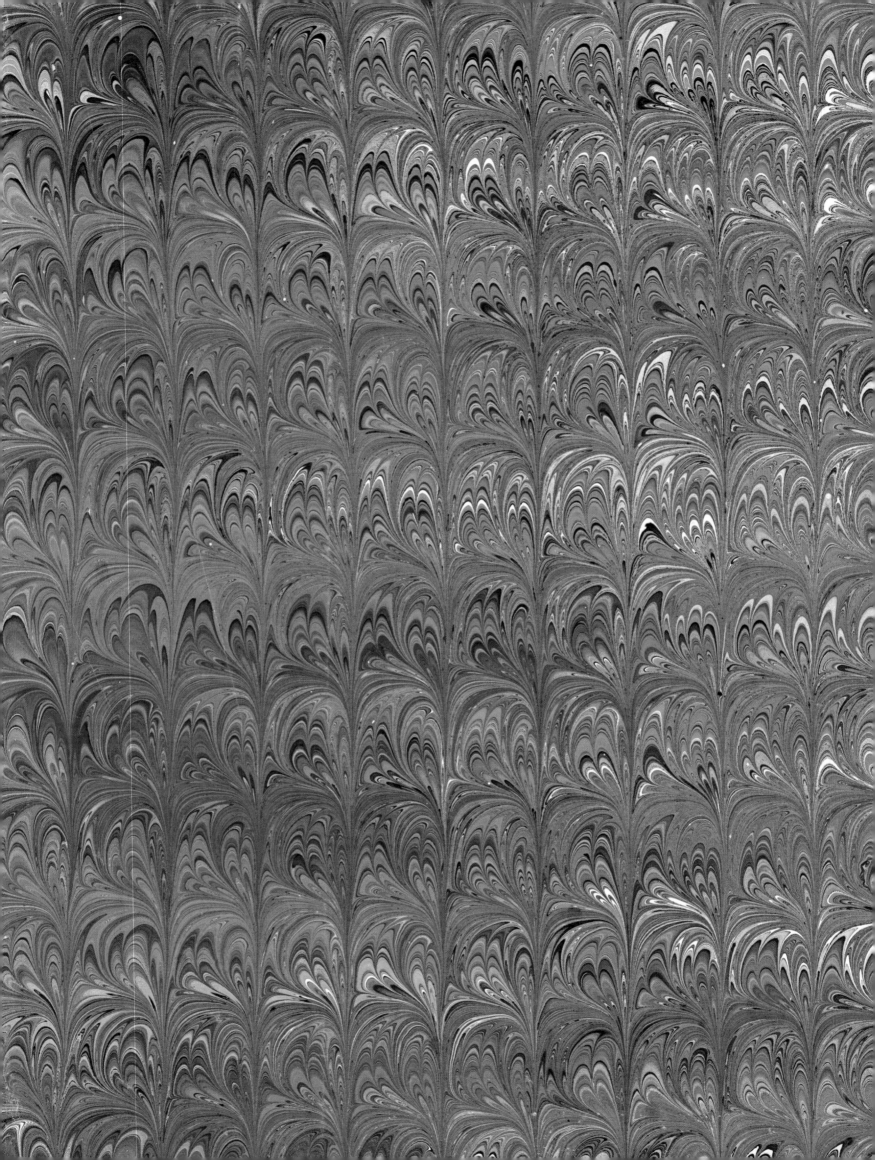